LEOMON'S CHALLENGE

John Whitman

HarperEntertainment

An Imprint of HarperCollins*Publishers*

HarperEntertainment
An Imprint of HarperCollins*Publishers*
10 East 53rd Street, New York, NY 10022

HarperCollins books are available at special quantity discounts for bulk purchases for sales promotions, premiums, or fund-raising. For information, please call or write: Special Markets Department, HarperCollins Publishers Inc., 10 East 53rd Street, New York, NY 10022. Telephone: (212) 207-7528. Fax: (212) 207-7222.

ISBN 0-06-107189-7

First printing: October 2000

Printed in the United States of America

Visit HarperEntertainment on the World Wide Web at
www.harpercollins.com

❖ 10 9 8 7 6 5 4 3 2 1

It was cold on File Island. The temperature had been dropping steadily, and a frigid wind blew through the forests and down the island's data paths.

That freezing wind also chilled the bones of the seven human children walking along a path near the island's central mountain. The children had no way of knowing if this frigid weather was unusual. In fact, they didn't even know how they'd arrived on that mysterious island. One day at summer camp they had simply been whisked away to this place, which seemed nothing like Earth. There they met seven small creatures called Digital Monsters, or Digimons, for short.

With the help of their Digimon friends, the children searched for a way off the island and back home, but so far they'd done nothing but encounter larger—and sometimes meaner—Digimons. Digimons ranged in size from the smaller "Rookies" that had befriended the kids, to larger Rookie Digimons, and enormous Champion Digimons with incredible powers. Luckily for the seven castaway kids, their own Digimons had the power to digivolve up to more powerful levels, but only if they were inspired by the courage and strength of their new companions.

All this made for a bewildering adventure. And now, to make things worse, they were freezing.

"Ooh, I can't take this cold," said a boy named Joe, who had a habit of complaining.

His Digimon partner, a furry creature

named Gomamon, snapped back, "I know this is no day at the beach, Joe, but that's no reason to be a worry-wart about it. Pardon the pun, but *chill out*. Besides, only you have a problem with the cold."

The others were too busy shivering to answer.

Gomamon sighed. "Okay, everyone, think warm!"

The leader of the group, a boy named Tai, tried to keep a stiff upper lip. He jabbed his hands into his pockets and said with a shrug, "Ah, come on, you guys, the cold isn't that bad!"

The most computer-oriented human member of the group, a boy nicknamed Izzy, looked at Tai in disbelief. "Maybe not if you'rc a polar bear or a penguin!" he said.

Tai laughed. "Yeah, but if it snows, we'll throw some snowballs."

"And make snowmen." Mimi, a girl dressed all in pink, said with a laugh.

One of the Digimons, an insectlike creature called Tentomon, looked at Gomamon and whispered, "What is 'Snowmon?'"

Gomamon shrugged. "Probably a Digimon from their planet."

Izzy laughed. "It's difficult to explain."

"The best thing about snowballs," said Izzy, "is that you can throw them at each other. It's a fun game we play during the winter!"

Matt, who was always

the coolest kid even in winter, laughed. "Yeah, we could even build a snow fort."

Tai sensed a challenge. "You'll need one," he said playfully.

Not to be outdone, a girl named Sora jumped in. "I bet I could beat you both blindfolded."

Beside her, the youngest member of the group, T.K., looked around for the snow everyone was talking about. "I want to build an igloo."

Joe shook his head. "Come on, guys, get serious. It would be horrible if it started snowing right now."

Sora sighed. "Lighten up a little, Joe. We're just trying to look on the positive side of things."

Joe groaned.

T.K. was still looking around for the snow. "When's it gonna snow, Tai?"

Tai felt goose bumps on his arms. "Probably any second now."

"Right on Joe's head." Matt laughed.

Joe glared at them all. "If the temperature drops any lower than it is already, we won't be able to camp out anymore—we'll be frozen digitreats."

The others laughed.

Joe felt himself get hot under the collar despite the cold. Ever since they'd been transported to this mysterious island, he'd been trying to tell them to be careful. But the others hardly ever listened to him, despite the fact that he was the oldest in the group.

"Go ahead and laugh," he said in disgust. "But when your tootsies freeze, don't come crying to me. I'll just say I told you so."

Gomamon felt something cold touch his nose and looked up. Small white flakes were falling from the sky. "Um, excuse me, what's that white stuff?"

Snow had, indeed, begun to fall. In just a few minutes it blanketed the ground, covering the island as far as the eye could see in a clean white sheet.

Sora bent down and picked up a handful of snow. All their joking now seemed a little out of place. "What now, gang?"

Tai studied the dark sky. "Well, I think we should keep going. We're not going to get anywhere just sitting around."

Matt looked down at his shoes, then out at the deepening field of snow. "If we walk across this field in our sneakers, our toes'll go numb."

Joe shook his head. "It's impossible to continue!"

The snow continued to fall heavily. As the seven kids and their Digimon friends stood there, white fluff began to cover their shoulders and heads.

Tai shook a frosty cap off his head. "So what are we supposed to do?" he said. "Just stand here? We either go across the field or climb up that big mountain."

A small dinosaur Digimon named Agumon suddenly lifted his nose and sniffed the air. "Whoa, there. Wait a sec. There's a weird odor in the air."

Biyomon, a pink birdlike Digimon, ruffled her feathers. "I do believe Agumon's right."

"What could it be?" wondered yet another Digimon, this one named Gabumon.

They all smelled it now—a sort of thick, sweet smell, almost like something cooking.

Tai scratched his head. "I don't know what it is, but it's something—"

"Something very familiar!" Izzy finished for him.

Biyomon flapped her wings excitedly. "Hey, it's steam!"

They heard a loud hissing sound and saw a cloud of steam rise up over the horizon.

"It must be a geyser," Joe guessed.

"Come on, let's go," Tai said.

Forgetting the cold, the kids and Digimons trudged across the field toward the rising steam. Passing through a line of trees, they discovered a pool of bubbling water. There was no snow anywhere around the shores of this little pond, and any that fell into the water melted instantly.

"It's a hot spring," T.K. said. "The water's naturally warm."

Mimi brightened up instantly. "Oh, that's perfect. I haven't taken a bath since we landed on this island."

"And we can get warm!" T.K. said.

But Tai frowned. They were still a dozen feet from the edge of the pool, and he was already sweating. "I think the water's too hot."

Tentomon sidled closer to the water and nodded. "We'd be cooked if we jumped in this."

"Well, technically, we'd be boiled," Izzy pointed out.

Mimi looked crushed. "There go my dreams of a nice, warm bath."

Mimi's Digimon, Palmon, had the graceful look of a plant. She leaned over the water and breathed deeply. "Too bad. The water looks so inviting."

Matt chuckled. "Yeah, it *would* be inviting if you were a vegetable!"

Joe, miserable as usual, couldn't understand why the others worried about taking a bath. "Hey, what's a little dirt compared to starving? We need to find something to eat, and there's nothing in sight."

Little T.K.'s eyes lit up, and he yelled, "Oh yes, there is!"

"Hmm?" Joe said, "What are you talking about? There's nothing around here but a bunch of rocks and boiling pond water."

"And snow," Sora said. "Don't forget lots of snow."

"But look!" T.K. said.

The other children followed his line of sight until their eyes came to rest on an object standing on the far side of the water.

Matt's usually supercool expression twisted in complete surprise. "Is that what I think it is?"

"I hope so," Mimi said. "And my stomach hopes so, too."

It was a refrigerator—a tall, white, perfectly normal refrigerator that would have looked right at home in any kitchen. But it wasn't in a kitchen; it was standing in the middle of an open field next to a hot spring on a mysterious island in DigiWorld.

"Tell me I'm not imagining this," said Joe.

"It's for real," Tai said. "It's got to be."

Joe remained skeptical. They'd already seen so many amazing things on this island that his brain was about to burst with all the impossibilities. When they first arrived on the island, they'd discovered a beach lined with hundreds of pay telephones. But every time they tried to use one, all they got was a ridiculous recording. And that was just on the first day! Things hadn't gotten any more normal since.

"Ah, come on, that's ridiculous! What would a refrigerator be doing out here?"

13

Matt chuckled. "Well, back home don't you always keep the refrigerator running?"

"Sure."

"Maybe this one ran all the way here!" Matt laughed.

Little T.K. rubbed his stomach. "Where there's a fridge, there's usually food."

"But–" Joe still protested.

"We'll never know until we try," Sora pointed out.

The humans and Digimons hurried over to the refrigerator. "Ready?" Tai said. He reached forward to grab the handle.

3

The children held their breath as Tai pulled the door open. On File Island, there was no telling what they might find.

The door swung open and the children gasped.

"Eggs," Tai said, looking inside. "Lots of eggs."

Agumon snorted, "There must be a zillion of 'em!"

Tai's stomach growled. "Yeah! Grub on! This food will keep us all stuffed for a month!"

Joe jumped in the way, his arms spread out in warning. "Wait a minute! You shouldn't even touch them. We don't know if they're fit for human consumption."

Tai rolled his eyes. "Then I'll be the guinea pig. If I turn purple, you'll know they're not edible."

But Joe was tired of the others not listening to him. He had a right to his opinion, and since he was the oldest in the group, he thought the others ought to pay more attention to it. "There's more to it than that, Tai," he argued. "Even if they are edible, they don't belong to us. Taking them would make us thieves. You've got to think about stuff like that, Tai."

Matt cast an eye toward their surroundings. "Unless you're into eating rocks, we don't have too much choice."

Sora frowned. She didn't like the idea of stealing, either, but her rumbling stomach didn't seem to care. "I'm sure whoever owns these eggs would say yes if they knew we were in trouble."

Izzy nodded. "This is an emergency situation."

Tentomon buzzed, "Mm-hm. Rationalize away."

Joe grunted in agreement.

But the other adventurers and the Digimons had begun to cook the eggs. Agumon had used his Pepper Breath to help start a fire, and Biyomon flapped her wings to keep it going as Sora cooked the eggs on a flat stone.

They used the hot spring to make hard-boiled eggs out of some others. While the other children carved chopsticks out of twigs, the Digimons used their strong claws to cut bowls out of the rocks.

Sora leaned over her makeshift stone stove. "Sunny-side-up eggs are my specialty!"

A few minutes later, almost everyone had a bowl full of eggs in front of them. "Yummy!" said Mimi. "These are so gourmet!"

Sora tried to give some eggs to Joe, but he didn't feel like eating.

"I'm sorry," he said, "this just makes me uncomfortable. We'd be in big trouble if someone got sick. It's not like we can call an ambulance on this island."

Tai was already wolfing down his eggs. "Oh, boy! I haven't had a meal like this in a long time. My stomach is chiming!"

Matt nodded. "Yeah, if there was some ketchup to go with this, it'd be perfect."

"I love ketchup and eggs, too!" his little brother T.K. said.

"That," Sora said, "sounds gross."

Gomamon shuffled over to Joe. "What's the matter, Joe?"

Joe sighed. "Oh, I was just thinking that if we were home, ketchup wouldn't be a problem. I'm just homesick, I guess."

Mimi stopped eating and her face fell into a sad look. "Now I'm homesick, too. How depressing."

Matt counted on his fingers. "It's been four days since we've been here. I wonder if anybody's trying to find out where we are."

"*We* can't even find out where we are," Tai pointed out. He glanced up and saw the tall peak of the island's central mountain rising high above them.

Sora said, "Cheer up! Tell me how you like your eggs and I'll do my very best."

Joe shrugged. "I prefer them to be covered in salt and pepper, but I guess it doesn't matter."

Tai said, "How about soy sauce."

Matt said, "How about salsa!"

Sora groaned. "How about a reality check."

T.K. laughed. "And I'll have mine with mustard and jelly beans!"

Thinking they were serious, Mimi looked at the others. "You are all very weird. The only way to have eggs is with maple syrup and some-times cherries on top."

Sora's face nearly turned green. "Now *that* is weird."

Joe looked nearly as sick. "Uh, now I don't have any appet-ite at all."

Gomamon came up behind him. "Come on, Joe, they're just having fun."

Matt said, "Yeah, Joe! Lighten up!"

Tai shook his head. "You know, I think it's really too late for him. I don't think Joe is into the same things we are."

Joe glared at Tai, then said to Gomamon, "Well, really, cherries on eggs. That's just crazy talk. I like salt and pepper on eggs. Keep it simple, that's my motto."

Gomamon sniffed and shook his furry head. "I guess you're not the kind of guy that's meant to be adaptable."

Joe looked shocked. Gomamon was supposed to be his friend. He thought the

Digimon would take his side. "What do you mean?"

Gomamon baited Joe. "Let's face it, Joe. You're kind of a stick in the mud, if you get my drift."

"I'm just practical!" Joe protested. By this time he was standing up, towering over Gomamon.

"You're stuffy!" Gomamon snapped back.

The other kids had gotten involved in another discussion and didn't notice that Joe and Gomamon were arguing.

Joe felt his face turn red. "Well, someone around here has to have a head on his shoulders!" He took a step toward Gomamon.

Gomamon's fur stiffened. "You want to fight?"

"Sure!" Joe said. Angrily, he charged at Gomamon.

4

The others heard the angry voices and rushed over in time to pull Joe and Gomamon apart. Matt held on to Joe. "Hey, hey! You'd better calm down."

"I *am* calm!" Joe shrieked. "He's the one who's dingy! And he hurt my arm."

"Well, look, we have a bigger argument going on," Matt said. "While you were talking with Gomamon, we were trying to figure out what to do next."

"Yeah," Tai said, "and we figured out that Matt's a big chicken!"

"I am not!" Matt protested.

Joe blinked. He'd been so involved in his own troubles, he

hadn't realized that the others were arguing, too. "What's going on?" he asked.

Izzy explained. "Matt and Tai are debating whether or not we should climb Infinity Mountain over there." He pointed to the enormous peak.

Tentomon looked up, and up, to the peak high among the clouds. "Infinity Mountain is a doozy, that's for sure."

Tai said, "Yeah, but it's a perfect spot. It's the best view of the island."

Matt shook his head. "Nobody would make it up to that peak. It's too much of a gamble."

Biyomon puffed up her feathers. "And there are lots of ferocious Digimons on that mountain."

"Don't be such wimps!" Tai said.

Matt scowled at him. "You can't put everybody in danger just to get a view of the island. There's got to be a better solution." He

25

looked at Joe. "What's your opinion on this?"

Joe was startled. Usually, Matt and Tai both disagreed with his ideas. This was the first time he'd been asked to decide on an argument between them. "Um," he said, trying to think. "I, uh, I think Tai's right about going up to the peak."

"Ha!" Tai said victoriously.

"But," Joe added, "Matt brought up a really good point. It'd be kind of dumb to lead everybody to a place we don't know much about."

Sora looked up at the sky. "Well, whatever we do, let's do it, because it's getting dark."

Agumon yawned. "I think we ought to get a little shut-eye."

Gabumon agreed. "That's right, there'll be plenty of time to argue in the morning."

Sora had spotted some caves in the distance, and the group sought shelter there. Inside a small cave, they all curled up with their Digimons to keep warm, and soon they were fast asleep.

Everyone, that is, except Joe.

He couldn't sleep. He was still thinking about the moment when Tai and Matt had asked him for his opinion. It was his chance to prove that, as the oldest, he was a leader. But all he'd done was agree with both of them instead of making a decision.

Now, lying awake, he thought, *Someone's going to get hurt if I don't do something fast. But how? I couldn't even end the argument. That wasn't very smart. I'm the oldest. I'm responsible for everyone.*

Joe stood up and quietly left the cave. It was cold outside, but clear, and he could see the shadow of Infinity Mountain rising above him. "The others aren't cautious enough. They might get hurt. I have to do this myself."

"What are you up to, Joe?"

Joe whirled around to find Gomamon staring at him. "You're not thinking of climbing that mountain by yourself, are you?"

"You're not going," Joe stated. "You're absolutely not going with me."

The only thing harder to escape than an angry Digimon was a friendly Digimon who wanted to protect you. So a few minutes later, Joe and Gomamon were walking together.

The climb up Infinity Mountain started out tough, and it got tougher with each step. After an hour of climbing, Joe was exhausted. He struggled to pull himself up while, beside him, Gomamon jumped from spot to spot with ease.

"You getting tired, Joe?" the Digimon said. "I can give you a hand."

Joe looked at Gomamon's monstrous paw. "You call that a hand?"

Gomamon's eyes flashed angrily until he realized it was a joke. "Wow, Joe, you might have a sense of humor after all."

Suddenly, the mountain began to rumble.

Joe grabbed a rock to keep from falling. "Oh, wow, is this mountain a volcano?"

Gomamon said, "No, I don't think—"

"Look!" Joe cried.

Above them, a great hole had suddenly opened up in the side of the mountain. A moment later, a swarm of dark, round objects wheeled out into the sky. But instead of falling, they seemed to be flying this way and that, as though searching for something.

"The Black Gears!" Gomamon said fearfully.

They'd encountered Black Gears before.

Keeping the peace isn't easy when
Matt and Tai go at it.

"We make quite a
team," said Gomamon.

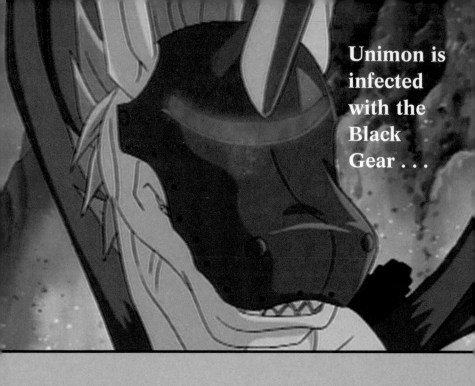

Unimon is infected with the Black Gear . . .

. . . and he keeps Joe and Gomamon on the edge!

Joe saves the day!

Joe is lucky to have a friend like
Ikkakumon to fall back on!

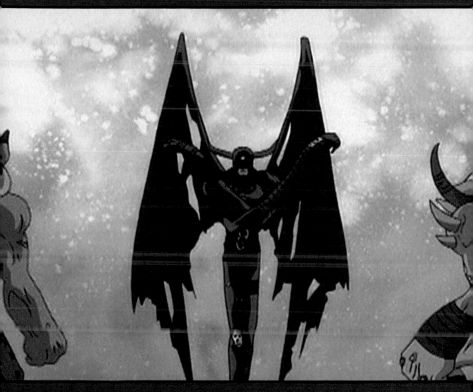

Evil shows his face.

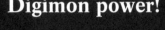
Digimon power!

The kids and their Digimons are not going
to take their separation lying down!

But will they ever be reunited after
Devimon breaks apart File Island?

Digivice to the rescue again.

Has Devimon finally gotten
what he wants? Destruction
of the Digidestined!

Mysterious and powerful, these terrible objects appeared out of nowhere and imbedded themselves into the bodies of the island's many Digimons. When that happened, even the wisest, kindest Digimon suddenly turned evil.

"The Gears come from the top of the mountain," Joe said. "We'll have to climb up there and see."

Gomamon looked at his friend in surprise. Joe was usually the one to run *away* from danger, not *toward* it. Maybe there was hope for him after all.

They found a trail and began to walk along it when, suddenly, they heard a sound like a horse's whinny. Rounding a corner on the mountain, they found themselves staring at a huge winged horse with a helmet on his head topped by a sharp horn. The creature

looked like a flying unicorn. He was swooping down toward the side of the mountain.

"Who's that?" Joe whispered.

"That's Unimon!" Gomamon said happily. "He's a very wise old Digimon. I like him!"

Unimon landed gently on a ledge near a small waterfall and began to drink.

"What a beautiful horse," Joe said.

"See, I told you, Unimon wouldn't hurt a fly," Gomamon said. "Hey, maybe he can tell us what we need to know."

Gomamon started forward. "Hey, Unimon! It's me, Gomamon! Can you help us?"

The giant horse looked up at them as though it was about to respond. But at that moment a strange sound, which was echoing off the mountain walls, filled their ears. It was a high-pitched throbbing sound, and it was growing louder by the second.

They all looked up in time to see something flash out of the sky—something dark, ominous, and swift.

"Black Gear!" Joe called out in warning.

Too late. The Black Gear plunged into

Unimon's back, sticking there like an evil thorn. Unimon screamed and reared back.

"Do you think he's in trouble?" Joe asked.

Hearing Joe's voice, Unimon turned on them, the eyes behind his helmet blazing angrily.

"Uh, I think we're the ones in trouble!" Gomamon said.

5

The sun was just rising over the hilltops when Sora woke up. With a yawn she got up and walked outside the cave. The weather had improved during the night, and she stretched as she felt the sun warm her skin.

As she finished her stretch she glanced down and saw some writing scratched into the ground in front of the cave.

I'LL BE BACK IN A LITTLE WHILE. PLEASE WAIT FOR ME. JOE.

Sora glanced up at Infinity Mountain.

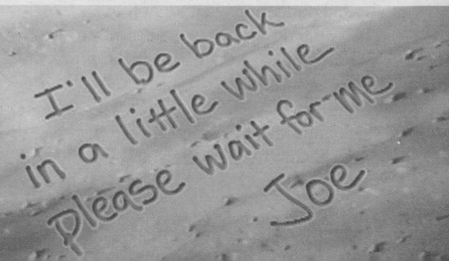

Had Joe tried to climb that thing by himself?

"Everybody wake up!" she called out. "We have an emergency!"

On the mountainside, Joe and Gomamon ran for their lives. Unimon had launched himself into the air on his great wings and swooped dangerously close to them.

The Digimon opened his mouth and blasted with an Aerial Attack, a powerful ball of pure energy. It struck the mountain beside them.

Rocks and dirt shattered, nearly throwing Joe and Gomamon off the side of a cliff. As quickly as he could, Joe picked himself up and lifted his Digimon out of a pile of rubble. "You've got to do something!"

"What?" the little Digimon asked.

Unimon hovered above the path before them. Behind, the ledge had been shattered by his power blast. Joe and Gomamon cowered together on the narrow rock ledge, bracing themselves for what was to come. There was nowhere for them to run, and they knew Unimon wasn't going to give up his attack until they were destroyed.

"Ready for another Aerial Attack?" the Digimon Champion said. He opened his mouth again

Joe closed his eyes. He knew there was nothing he could do.

But just as Unimon was about to fire, they heard a high-pitched shriek, and out of nowhere, Birdramon appeared. Birdramon was the Champion that Biyomon digivolved into, and she was very strong. She slammed into Unimon and pinned him to the mountainside.

Tai, Sora, and Agumon had hitched a ride on Birdramon's legs, and now they jumped off to see if Joe and Gomamon were all right, while Birdramon held Unimon down.

But Birdramon was not quite strong enough. With a shrug, Unimon threw her off. "Aerial Attack!" he called out, blasting Birdramon with his powerful energy spheres. Stunned by the blow, Birdramon tumbled down the side of the mountain.

"Birdramon!" Sora called out, sliding down after her friend.

Tai looked at Agumon. "Well?"

Agumon nodded. A shaft of brilliant light surrounded him as he called out, "Agumon digivolve to . . . Greymon!"

Instantly, the small Digimon transformed

into the giant Champion Greymon, a huge two-legged dinosaur with a horned head. Powerful Greymon charged at the winged horse, but Unimon was too quick. He slipped away, then whirled around and smashed Greymon down against the stones

"Greymon, you okay?" Tai asked desperately.

Just then, the Champion took the full force of Unimon's Aerial Attack on his chest. Snarling, Greymon unleashed his fiery Nova Blast in reply.

But Unimon was simply too fast, dodging the fireball in midair and striking back with his own powerful energy weapon. This time Greymon dodged the shot, but the Aerial Attack still smashed against the mountain, throwing them all off their feet.

"Tai and Greymon are in big trouble," Gomamon said.

"It's worse than that!" Joe said. "Unimon is going after Sora and Birdramon!"

The winged horse had already swooped down to a lower slope where Sora knelt

next to the stunned bird Digimon. As the attacking creature approached, Birdramon gathered her strength and leaped up. "Meteor Wing!" she called out, sending bolts of energy at Unimon. The winged horse slipped away and drove its horned head right against Birdramon's body, dropping her to the ground.

On the broken ledge above, Joe saw Unimon flying beneath him as he wheeled around for a final pass. Looking down, he could see the Black Gear imbedded in the Digimon's back.

"The Gear!" he said. "I'll get it."

He inched to the edge of the cliff, and as Unimon passed beneath him, he said, "This is crazy!" and he jumped.

Joe landed hard on the giant horse's back, but he held on. Crawling forward, he grabbed hold of the Black Gear and pulled.

"Oh, no! It won't budge!"

Unimon screamed and started to buck in midair, nearly throwing Joe into oblivion.

"Joe, don't try to be a hero!" Gomamon called out.

"Yeah!" Joe called back. "Well, I've got to do this one thing!"

He pulled again, but the Gear was stuck fast to the Digimon's body. "I won't give

up until I do this. I won't!" he yelled.

But Unimon bucked again, and this time he managed to throw Joe off. The boy hurtled through the air, head over heels, and fell straight toward the jagged rocks at the base of the mountain.

As he fell, a flash of intense light covered the mountainside, surrounding Gomamon. The small Digimon, connected to Joe by a magical bond of friendship, had responded to his friend's incredible act of courage.

In that instant, the small Rookie vanished, replaced by the huge form of a furry, horn-headed Champion, as the creature called out, "Gomamon digivolve to... Ikkakumon!"

In a flash the Digimon Champion darted forward, catching Joe on his thick, furry back.

"What?" Joe said in surprise.

"Hold on, Joe, 'cause we're going for a ride!" Ikkakumon growled.

Seeing this new threat, Unimon swooped down again, firing his powerful Aerial Attack. But Ikkakumon wasn't just huge, he was fast, and slipped away easily.

"Harpoon Torpedo!" he called out, lowering his head. From the single horn on his skull, Ikkakumon released a series of fiery rockets. A swarm of them streaked into the sky, but Unimon managed to dodge them all.

"He's much too fast!" Joe wailed.

"We'll see," Ikkakumon replied.

Even as he spoke, the fiery rockets broke apart, revealing smaller rockets that swerved

around and exploded against Unimon, knocking the startled Champion to the ground.

Instantly, he leaped to his feet again and flew away. But as he flapped his wings, the Black Gear came loose, shattered by Ikkakumon's attack. Then it vanished into thin air.

"Ikkakumon!" Joe called out. "You saved the day!"

Unimon, stunned and bewildered, flashed across the sky with a flap of his huge wings, and was gone.

Joe and Ikkakumon turned back to the

others, and found Sora, Tai, Birdramon, and Greymon uninjured. As the threat of attack vanished, all the Champion Digimons returned to their Rookie forms: Agumon, Biyomon, and Gomamon.

"Joe, you were awesome out there!" Tai said. "You were so great, you made Gomamon digivolve! You're a pretty cool dude after all!"

"That's not why I did it," Gomamon said with a casual yawn. "I just didn't want Joe to fall on his head."

Tai looked up at the mountainside. "You know, we're almost there. Let's find the top!"

Together, they climbed the last stretch to

the heights of Infinity Mountain. When they reached the peak, they found themselves looking out over the entire island.

But there was nothing else there. No land in sight. No other islands. Just miles of ocean, and File Island sitting by itself in the middle, with them on it.

Tai sighed. "Well, I guess we came all this way, and we didn't find anything."

Joe shrugged, thinking of the courage he'd found. "Well, there's nothing at the top," he agreed. "But I think I found something on the way."

6

The seven children and their Digimons stood at the very top of File Island, looking down on the land to which they'd been mysteriously transported. Joe peered over the edge, thinking about the long hike back to the base of the mountain.

"This place sure could use a good bus system."

"Yeah," Matt said, "but it looks like we're at the end of the line."

On the far side of the mountain, a powerful Digimon named Leomon prowled along a cliffside path. Tall, broad-shouldered, with the head of a lion and a tremendous sword at his waist, he looked menacing. But he was, in fact, one of the most powerful of the good Digimons.

As a high-pitched sound reached his sharp ears, Leomon ducked low. His keen eyes spotted a dark object race across the sky, and he recognized it instantly.

"Another Black Gear." He watched it disappear, but a sense of uneasiness remained with him. "I sense danger," he growled.

Even as he spoke, a horrible green-skinned figure leaped down from a cliff above and landed on the path before him. The creature had thick arms and legs, a huge head covered with wiry hair, and it carried a club the size of a tree.

"Leomon!" the creature bellowed. "You may be the mightiest of the good Digimons,

but now you face me. Your kind-hearted leadership doesn't impress me!"

A low growl issued from Leomon's throat. "Ogremon! You are truly the most evil of the bad Digimons. There's no limit to your ruthlessness."

As if to prove the point, Ogremon attacked, bringing his massive club crashing down. Leomon blocked it with his sword and, with one quick move, flicked the club from Ogremon's hand, but he lost his own sword in doing so.

Weaponless now, the two Champions faced each other. Ogremon snorted, "No

one asked you here. No one wants you here. I strongly suggest that you go, now, while you still can!"

Leomon roared, "The endless attack of Black Gears comes from this mountain! They're transforming perfectly peaceful and innocent Digimons into ferocious monsters. And I have come here to make it stop!"

"You've been warned!" Ogremon bellowed.

The two Digimons charged, exchanging blows powerful enough to shatter stone. Ogremon lashed out with a powerful energy blast, but Leomon countered with his terrible "Fist of the Beast King." The two energy

beams struck each other, shaking the mountain to its roots.

The two enemies gathered themselves for another round, but a deep, booming voice rolled over them. "Both of you, stop! Cease this foolishness! I command that the two of you work together for me, not fight!"

Leomon looked around, trying to find the source of the disembodied voice. He snarled, "I'll never work with him!"

"And I won't work with him!" Ogremon said.

"Be silent!"

Out of nowhere, a dark figure appeared

before them, shifting like a shadow out of the ground until it stood tall and looming. It was black, with long arms like claws, and a grim face.

"You will do as I say," the dark figure said. "For I am Devimon, ultimate ruler of the demon Underworld. You must obey my every command."

Ogremon snorted, "You don't need this joker. I can handle anything you want done without anyone's assistance."

"I think not," Devimon said. "It is the Digidestined kids you'll be fighting."

"The Digidestined?" Ogremon said in surprise. "Where are they?"

Devimon sneered impatiently. "They're already here on Infinity Mountain. Now go find them and destroy them immediately."

Leomon lashed his tail. "Destroy *them*? I'll destroy you for threatening the Digidestined. Fist of the Beast King!" He punched his hand forward, setting loose a powerful energy blast.

But as it approached Devimon, the evil Digimon seemed to fade away. From nowhere, his cold voice spoke. "Freeze, Leomon. I am not requesting your cooperation, I am demanding it. Prepare for the Touch of Evil."

Unseen by Leomon, a long hand shot up out of the ground behind him and touched his neck. Dark energy surrounded him. Leomon screamed in agony, then fell silent.

Devimon appeared, floating up out of the ground like a ghost. "Now you will obey my every command."

In a low, strained voice, Leomon replied, "Yes. I will obey."

7

On the high peak of Infinity Mountain, Tai used a small spyglass he carried to study the shores of the island. He stopped to draw a rough map on a piece of paper.

Nearby, Joe sat with his head in his hands. His earlier show of courage had faded, replaced by exhaustion. "We don't need a map to know we're totally lost. I figured that out a long time ago."

Beside him, Mimi had her mind on a different plane of thought. "I just figured out that these gloves don't really go with this dress."

"They really don't," Palmon agreed.

Grrrrrrrr.

The noise that reached them sounded like thunder, if thunder could be bottled into a single threatening tone.

They all turned to find the imposing lion-like shape of Leomon standing on the path.

"Uh-oh," Joe said.

The Rookie Patamon laughed. "Don't worry, that's Leomon. He's our friend."

T.K. swallowed. "A friend with very big teeth."

Patamon said, "Oh, he just uses them for smiling."

Gabumon agreed. "He's a just leader. And a role model for all Digimons."

"I want the children," Leomon snarled.

"Um, that's a role model?" Matt asked.

Gabumon shifted nervously. "Something is very wrong here."

Leomon drew his sword.

"Run!" Sora shouted. "Run! This way!"

They spotted another path leading down the mountain,

and the children and their Digimons raced down the slope with Joe in the lead.

They were halfway down, and beginning to breathe sighs of relief, when another Digimon appeared, blocking the path. It was Ogremon. "And just where do you think you're going?"

The children were trapped.

"D-does Ogremon look hungry to you?" Patamon wondered aloud.

T.K. whimpered. "We're too small to eat. And I'm full of junk food."

"I don't think he'd mind a little snack," Gomamon wailed.

Behind them, Leomon said, "Make it easy on yourselves. Give up now. Or else!"

Matt looked around. "I don't see an exit door."

"This proves the theorem," Izzy observed,

"that properly executed teamwork works. Even for the bad guys."

Biyomon looked confused. "But Leomon's always been Ogremon's worst enemy. What happened to them?"

Ogremon and Leomon charged.

But the Digimon friends would not give up without a fight. In response to the attackers, the six smaller Digimons transformed to the next level, becoming larger, stronger, more powerful. Only Patamon had remained in Rookie form.

Leomon leaped toward them, but Greymon threw him back with a thrust of his

horned head, and Ogremon was driven back by Ikkakumon's strength.

Greymon released a Nova Blast that kept Leomon off balance, while Togemon let loose a vicious Needle Spray that peppered the lionlike monster with stinging barbs.

On the other side of the path, Ikkakumon fired his Harpoon Torpedo. Breaking apart in midflight, the explosive tip slammed right into Ogremon, stunning him.

High above and unseen, Devimon watched it all. "They've all digivolved. They've learned the secret of teamwork. This group of six attacking together is quite dangerous. But I wonder why Patamon has not digivolved?"

Below, the Digimons prepared a second assault, but just as they gathered them-

selves, they heard a rumble. Looking up, they saw tons of rock break loose from the cliffside, tumbling down toward them.

"Avalanche!" Joe called out. There was nowhere to run. They'd be crushed!

But the Digimons were there to protect them. "Nova Blast!" "Meteor Wing!" "Howling Blaster!" "Electroshocker!" The sound of the Digimons firing their energy weapons was earsplitting. The multiple blasts slammed into the approaching rocks, turning tons of stone into fine powder that drifted gently down onto the children.

Tai blinked. "Everybody okay?"

Matt said sarcastically, "Sure. Like a day at the beach."

"What's wrong with the Digimons?" T.K. asked.

Tai whirled around to see that the Digimons had digivolved back to their smaller forms. Even as he watched, they collapsed on the ground and did not move.

"Agumon! What's wrong?"

The little dinosaur Digimon lifted his head weakly. "We're not hurt, Tai. Just a little tired."

"You've digivolved twice in one morning. No wonder," Tai said. He looked around. "Did anyone see what happened to the bad guys?"

Gabumon barely managed to stand. He looked over the edge of the cliff. "Do you think the avalanche knocked them both off the cliff?"

Joe, too, looked over the edge. The bottom was still far, far below them. "Unless they could fly, they're both goners."

"They might be able to fly," Sora said. "Anything's possible in this place."

"Something else is bothering me," Tai said. "What set off that avalanche?"

Izzy gave the textbook answer. "Stress accumulates until ultimately a crack develops from the pressure and suddenly terra firma isn't so firma."

Tai wasn't convinced. "You think so? I thought maybe something blasted it loose."

The children and Digimons continued on down the path.

Behind them, unseen, Devimon observed his enemies. "They are more powerful than I suspected, but I shall strike while they are exhausted, and destroy them all."

The group of adventurers reached the bottom of the mountain safely and walked under the cover of the trees.

Izzy, who loved to analyze everything, said, "I'm intrigued that our Digimons underwent two digivolutions in a single day."

Tai laughed. "Yeah, well lucky for us they did!"

Sora added, "I think the Digimons are growing stronger. I wonder if that's a normal part of the process, or if we're bringing something special to them?"

Matt said, "I think it was too much for them."

"Palmon's looking very tired," Mimi agreed.

Palmon straightened up. "Hey, I've been tired before, Mimi. Don't worry!"

Tai said, "Rest sounds like a good idea for everyone."

"Rest where?" Sora groaned. "Last night we slept in a cave. I don't want to sleep on the ground."

"Why don't we sleep there?" Joe said, his voice filling with astonishment. "Look!"

Through the trees they saw a vision as amazing as anything they'd discovered yet on File Island.

It was a house. An enormous, spotless, lavish mansion set in the middle of a forest, on an island that contained no other human beings that they knew of.

"A mansion," Joe said.

"Maybe it's a hotel," Tai suggested. "Come on!"

Together they rushed forward. "I believe

we've found other life," Izzy said, noting their surroundings. "I mean, somebody had to have mowed the lawn."

"I hope thcy have a hot tub. Just so long as it's not too hot!" Joe said.

As the children rushed forward, it was Tai, oddly enough, who suddenly slowed down. Normally the first to run ahead, this time he felt more cautious. They'd certainly seen their share of strange things on the island . . . but a beautiful hotel, just when they'd hoped for a place to rest? That seemed not just weird, but too much of a coincidence.

"Wait, you guys," he said, "don't just go charging in. It might be dangerous."

"Maybe we should knock," Tai suggested.

"Nobody knocks on the door of a hotel!" Matt groaned.

"Well, here goes."
They opened the door

and stepped inside. The interior of the hotel was as beautiful as the exterior ... but it seemed empty. There was hardly any furniture. There was certainly no desk clerk.

"It looks weird," Tai said.

"It *feels* weird," Matt added.

Joe shrugged. He was just excited to be inside any building that looked even remotely like civilization. "Doesn't look weird or feel weird to me."

Izzy said, "I believe my definition of weird is different than yours."

Joe took a few more steps inside. "Think about it. Are we safer in the open woods, with no shelter, or here in a sturdy building we could defend from attack?"

Matt frowned. "He's got a point."

"Besides," Joe said, "look at the Digimons."

The seven little creatures stood wavering on their feet, their eyes half-closed. They were exhausted.

With no other options, the children and Digimons walked into the hotel, letting the doors close behind them.

9

Once they were inside the building, the feeling of emptiness grew stronger. Every footstep echoed. Every voice carried.

"Well, I guess we missed the summer rush," Tai said.

"Maybe this *is* the summer rush," Matt joked.

Tai shook his head. "This is one kooky, mixed-up world."

Gabumon lifted his head and sniffed. "Do you smell that?"

"What?"

"Food!" Gabumon howled happily, smacking his lips. "This way!"

The children raced after the Digimons, who sprinted at high speed down a long hallway. The hallway opened into a huge banquet room and there, set on a wide table, lay an enormous feast, with plates and huge bowls filled with every food they could imagine.

"Look at that spread!" Tai said, his mouth watering.

Matt's stomach rumbled, but he said, "Sorry for saying this everybody, but this looks like a setup."

The Digimons ignored him and scrambled up into some of the waiting chairs. Before

anyone could stop them, they began tearing into the food.

"Matt's right," Sora said. "This could be some sort of trap."

"Agumon," Tai asked his Digimon, "are you guys sure that food is safe to eat?"

In answer, Agumon tore off a chicken leg and bit into it with a loud chomp.

Joe rubbed his stomach. "That's it," he said at last. "I can't take it anymore. I'm gonna eat. If it's bad, then at least I won't die hungry!"

He practically jumped into a chair and began piling his plate with mashed potatoes, peas, carrots, and every kind of food he could lay his hands on. Unable to resist their own hunger, the others followed, until only Tai remained.

The boy sighed. "Oh, well. If one of us gets sick, we all get sick. I guess that's team-work, too."

In the next hour they said very few words besides, "Please pass the potatoes," or "Can you hand me another slice of salmon?"

By the time they'd eaten their fill, they had nearly stripped the table clean of food. Full and content, they searched the hotel until they found two adjoining bathing rooms with pools big enough for a dozen people.

The girls took one room and the boys took the other, and soon they were soaking in warm, relaxing water.

"Oh, this is perfect." Joe sighed, finally

washing days of File Island dirt off his body. "It's like a dream."

After they'd all bathed and dried off, they found a giant room filled with soft beds covered in clean sheets. Exhausted, each kid crawled into a bed and snuggled up next to his or her digifriend.

"Oh, I miss having a bed," Mimi sighed.

"I miss being home," Joe said. Then, catching the sad look that suddenly passed from person to person, he added, "Sorry for mentioning home, guys."

"That's okay, Joe," Tai said. "We all miss home."

Matt lay on his back, staring up at the ceiling. "I'll bet our disappearance caused a big fuss all over town. But we've been gone

so long, everybody must have given up looking for us." He yawned.

Sora followed his yawn with one of her own. Her voice drifted off as she said, "We'll find our way back. Don't worry."

"Let's just—" Mimi said, becoming drowsy "—let's just sleep."

And one by one, they drifted off.

As they slept, a dark shadow seeped in through a strange picture of an angel down-

stairs. In the middle of the lobby, the shadow formed into the figure of Devimon.

"It was so easy to deceive them! Even the Digidestined appear to have childishly

simple minds. Are you two ready?"

Out of the shadows stepped Ogremon and Leomon. The evil Digimon chortled, "What a pleasure to be rid of the Digidestined at last!"

Devimon smiled eagerly.

Above them, they heard footsteps carry down the hall. Tai had woken up, and Agumon had jumped up with him.

"Agumon," Tai groaned sleepily, "I can go to the bathroom by myself."

The little Digimon said cheerily, "I don't mind keeping you company, Tai. It's dark and scary here."

The boy said, "For your information, I

happen to like the dark. And please stop treating me like a—"

Before he could finish his sentence, the wall before him exploded. Through the hole stepped the muscled green figure of Ogremon. He had been waiting for them in the bathroom. "Now," the creature snarled, "I'm going to destroy you both."

"Ah!" Tai yelled. "Wake up, everybody! It's Ogremon!"

They turned to run . . . and found Leomon standing right behind them. "I must destroy you," the Champion growled.

10

Tai felt his knees shake and his tongue stick to the roof of his mouth, but he managed to mumble, "W-why do you hate me?"

Out of the darkness, an icy voice spoke. "He hates you because I commanded him to hate you."

Tai glanced around. Across the hallway he saw a figure move toward him. The shape was dark, a shade deeper than the darkness of the nearly empty building. Tai caught only a hint of long, leathery wings and a face twisted with evil.

Agumon gasped. "Get ready, Tai. Now the real trouble starts."

"Wh-who is that?" Tai said, trembling.

"That's Devimon. He's the guy who invented the nightmare."

Devimon smiled cruelly. "I have no need of this imaginary building."

The creature waved one long, gnarled hand. Instantly, the walls of the hotel vanished. Tai and Agumon found themselves standing under the open sky atop a jagged rock formation. Nearby, he could see the others still sleeping in their beds. But everything else—the banquet room, the baths, the hallways—was all gone.

Disturbed by the sudden change, Matt woke up. "Huh? Wake up, everybody! Something's wrong!"

As the others stirred, Devimon raised his hand again. "Because together you are strong, I will use my Touch of Evil to scatter you to the corners of the DigiWorld."

At his command, the beds in which they lay suddenly rose up and began spinning around in the air. Terrified, the kids and their Digimons clutched the bedposts to keep from being thrown out into the dark night sky.

"Agumon, we've got to do something!" Tai said.

"Tai," the Digimon gasped. "I . . . I'm too weak to walk. Even after eating all that food."

Devimon roared with laughter. "The food, the bath, the building. None of it was real. I created all of it in your imaginations."

Tai fought through his fear. "Listen, you! If you don't bring back my friends, you're gonna be in trouble!"

"Amusing," the evil Digimon laughed. "My concerns are much more important than your friends."

"Yeah, well they're my only concern," Tai said defiantly. "Bring them back now!"

Devimon stiffened, his fists forming into sharp claws. "You dare to order me? Let me show you who is in control here."

The demon Digimon raised his arms. With that single motion, the entire island began to tremble. In an instant, the stone foundation of the island cracked, and the entire landmass began to break apart.

"You see, I have discovered the secret of the Black Gears dwelling below. I call them forth to do my bidding!"

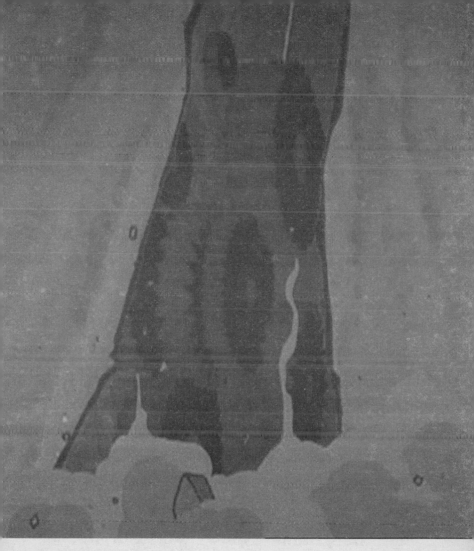

Infinity Mountain, as huge as it was, cracked straight down the middle and began to separate. At its core, Tai saw hundreds, perhaps thousands, of the Black Gears spinning, working their way through the island. As they spun, the isle continued to break apart, until a dozen separate pieces began to drift out into the sea.

Tai clung to a small piece of rock, his eyes half-shut, wishing he could plug his ears against the sound of the island being torn to pieces. And over that noise, he heard the evil voice of Devimon.

"You and your friends happened upon this tiny island, which is just one of the fragments of the Old World, scattered across an enormous ocean. You pretend you are strangers who know nothing about this, but I am aware that you are the Digidestined, who were sent to rescue this world from my domination!"

Tai felt his mouth go dry. "You got us wrong. We were just some kids at summer camp who got sucked into your world."

"Your lies no longer amuse me," Devimon said. "Leomon, bring an end to the Digidestined!"

Leomon nodded. "I will destroy them."

Bravely, Agumon jumped in front of Tai, gathered himself, and let loose his Pepper Breath. But he was weak, and the fire of his blast died before it ever reached the Champion Digimon.

Stepping forward, Leomon brushed Agu-

mon aside. "Yes," Devimon said. "Now the boy!"

Leomon grabbed Tai by the neck. Tai had never felt such a powerful grip in his life.

With his free hand, Leomon drew his sharp blade and raised it high.

11

Just before Leomon's blade came down, Sora came swooping helplessly by, still clinging to the bed that Devimon had set flying about the skies. As it did, something slipped from her pack and fell clattering to the ground. Small, metallic, with a bright circle at its center, Tai recognized it instantly. It was Sora's digivice.

Leomon heard the device land by his foot and looked down. As he did, the digivice came to life. Bright light shot forth, bathing Leomon in its rays. The Digimon roared in pain and surprise. As the light burned through him,

Tai and Agumon saw a dark shape melt out of Leomon's body and vanish.

"The Black Gear!" Agumon cheered. "The light drove it out of him!"

To Tai's relief, the monster dropped him.

"L-Leomon?" he asked. "Are you ... are you all right?"

The powerful creature shook his head as though trying to clear his mind. "I am free of Devimon's powers."

Tai picked up the digivice. "Do you know what this thing is?"

The heroic Digimon nodded. "I can tell you that for me it is proof that you are one of the Digidestined. In anyone else's hands, they are useless."

"And they will be useless still!" Devimon

roared. "When I have destroyed the children."

Raising his hand to the helpless kids floating around above him, Devimon poured forth his dark energy. Tentacles of power wrapped themselves around the children in the sky and began to drag them down swiftly, to be smashed against the ground.

But Leomon had fully recovered. "Fist of

the Beast King!" he roared. His energy bolt smashed against the ground on which Devimon stood. Spreading his wings, Devimon leaped into the air to avoid being crushed, but he lost his grip on the children as he did.

"Leomon is helping us!" Tentomon cheered. "We're going to be fine!"

"This isn't over, Leomon!" Devimon taunted. "Or have you forgotten your old friend?"

Ogremon came flying at him. But Leomon was just as swift, and he avoided the blow. Ogremon snarled, "Your soft heart is your weakness. We will never join as allies, and you will never know true power."

Leomon stepped back, pushing Tai and Agumon farther from Ogremon's reach. "You may defeat me," he said, "but the Digidestined will be out of your reach."

"No!" Tai said.

"Yes!" the lion Digimon roared. "Go now!"

Without waiting, the hero plunged his powerful blade into the ground. That single blow broke apart the ground on which Tai stood, carrying it away from Leomon and his enemies and into the watery channels created by the now-shattered island.

As Tai drifted farther from Leomon, he called out, "But why?"

"You're our last hope! Without you, my world doesn't stand a chance of survival. My own life means nothing!"

Seeing his chance, Ogremon leaped past Leomon, hurling himself out over the water toward Tai. But Leomon was ready. He punched forward with his energy fist and slapped Ogremon from the sky.

"You can escape, too!" Tai called out.

"I must prevent Devimon from pursuing you!" the Champion called out.

Tai's little island of rock was drifting away so rapidly that he could barely see Leomon now. His last image was a mere glimpse of the mighty Digimon turning back, just as Devimon fell on him like the shadow of death. Then they were out of sight.

A moment later Tai heard a single, strangled cry of agony. Then there was silence.

File Island had been shattered into pieces, each piece separated by the endless ocean of DigiWorld. But the high peak of Infinity Mountain stood untouched. And from its summit, Devimon surveyed his evil handiwork. Behind him stood his henchmen, Ogremon and Leomon, whom he had enslaved once again.

"The Digidestined survived our first encounter, but it won't be the last, I can promise them that." The evil Digimon turned to his servants. "They must not interfere with my plans. They must be destroyed. Will you do this for me, Leomon?"

Enslaved by Devimon's evil power, the heroic Digimon had no choice but to respond, "Your every order . . . I shall obey."